P9-ARY-701

CAM JANSEN
and the
Mystery at the
Monkey House

★ ★

DAVID A. ADLER
Illustrated by Susanna Natti

★ ★

A Dell Young Yearling Book

Published by
Dell Publishing
a division of
Bantam Doubleday Dell Publishing Group, Inc.
666 Fifth Avenue
New York, New York 10103

The trademark Yearling® is registered in the U.S. Patent and Trademark Office.

The trademark Dell® is registered in the U.S. Patent and Trademark Office.

ISBN: 0-440-40047-3

Reprinted by arrangement with Viking Penguin, Inc.

Printed in the United States of America

April 1988

10 9 8 7 6 5

WES

To my cousins
Chezki, Binyamin,
Sarah, and Batya

Chapter One

"Quick," Cam Jansen told her friend Eric Shelton. "Pull the cord. Ring the bell."

Cam and Eric were riding on a bus. Eric reached up and pulled the cord above his window. It rang a bell. The driver knew someone wanted to get off at the next stop. At the corner, the bus stopped and the driver opened the doors. Cam and Eric got off.

"We almost missed our stop," Cam said. "The Jackson Park Zoo is right up this block."

It was a cool spring afternoon. Cam and Eric had gone to the zoo right after school. When they reached the zoo entrance, Eric took out his wallet and paid the fee. Cam paid, too.

"Look," Eric said. He pointed to a boy just ahead. "There's Billy Adams. He's the boy I told you about. He just moved into my apartment building."

"Hey, Billy, Billy!" Eric called.

The boy turned. Cam and Eric walked

over to him. "This is my friend Jennifer Jansen," Eric told the boy. "But everyone calls her 'Cam'."

"Cam?"

"It's short for 'The Camera.' Everyone calls her that because she has an amazing memory. Her mind takes a picture of whatever she sees. When she wants to remember something, she just looks at the pictures she has stored in her brain."

Cam, Eric, and Billy were standing on a wide paved road. In front of them was a large map of the zoo.

Eric said, "Cam can take one look at this map. Then she can close her eyes and tell you where everything is."

"I don't believe it," Billy said.

Cam looked at the map. She said, "*Click*," and closed her eyes.

"What did she say?" Billy asked.

"*Click*," Eric whispered. "She always says that when she wants to remember something. It's the sound her mental camera makes when it takes a picture."

"Where are the giraffes?" Billy asked.

"Walk down this main road," Cam said with her eyes still closed. "When you pass the camel rides, turn right. First come the elephants, and then the giraffes."

"She's peeking," Billy said.

Cam turned around and said, "Now you can't say I'm peeking. Ask me another question."

Cam has red hair and freckles. Eric's hair is brown. Cam and Eric live near each other and are in the same fifth-grade class. Cam and Eric often walk to school together.

"Where's the Lion Safari Gift Shop?" Billy asked.

"It's on the main road right next to the Bear Hug Refreshment Stand."

Honk! Honk!

Cam opened her eyes. A large truck was on the road. Cam, Eric, and Billy moved

aside to let the truck pass. It was a gardener's truck. The back was filled with dirt, sticks, shovels, and rakes.

"Well, I'm smart, too," Billy said. "People think goats eat tin cans, but they don't. They just like to lick the glue off the labels. And the fastest animal is the cheetah."

"I didn't say Cam was smarter than you," Eric said. "I just said she has an amazing memory."

"I have a good memory, too. When I was two years old I met John and Jennie Hudson. They're friends of my parents. And I still remember their middle names. Jack and Donna."

"That's great," Eric said. "Now, let's go see the monkeys. They're always lots of fun."

Cam closed her eyes and said, *"Click."* Then she said, "To get to the monkey house, we just walk down the main path and make a left at the seal pool. The monkeys are right after the prairie dogs."

6

"Did you know that people in Malaysia train monkeys?" Billy asked. "They tie belts and long ropes on them. Then the monkeys climb trees and pick coconuts."

Eric smiled and said, "That's very interesting."

"Let's go," Cam said, as she walked ahead. "I don't want to *talk* about monkeys. I want to *see* them."

Chapter Two

There were very few people visiting the zoo. Cam, Eric, and Billy walked past the refreshment stand. The woman working there was reading a book. Nearby was a man with an ice-cream cart. He was sitting on a bench and resting.

As they walked past the seals, Billy said, "Did you know that baby seals can't swim? And do you know how seals keep warm? Their bodies are covered with lots of blubber. Blubber is fat."

"That's very interesting," Eric told Billy.

"I know that because I read lots of books about animals. I don't say '*Click*,' but I have a good memory. I remember what I read."

The monkey house was a large brick building. Outside the building, along both sides, were cages. Part of each cage was outside the monkey house and part was inside. Cam, Eric, and Billy walked into the building.

The monkey house smelled. And it was noisy.

Cam sat on a bench in the middle of the

house and looked from one cage to the next. Billy read the signs describing the different kinds of monkeys. Eric stood close to one of the cages and looked in.

Eric looked at the monkeys in the first cage. He stood with his hands behind his back. Cam noticed that a very small monkey was watching Eric. And the monkey was standing with his hands behind his back, too.

A monkey jumped onto a swing. Eric turned to look at it. The monkey watching Eric turned, too.

Eric watched the monkey swing. Then he walked to the next cage. When Eric walked, so did the very small monkey.

"Hey, Eric," Cam called. "You have a friend in that cage."

"What?"

Cam got off the bench. She pointed to the very small monkey and said, "That monkey is copying everything you do."

Eric looked at the monkey. The monkey

10

looked at Eric. Eric reached up and put his hands on his head. The monkey reached up, too. He put his hands on his head and smiled.

"Billy, come here," Cam whispered. "You have to see this."

Cam and Billy watched as Eric jumped. The monkey jumped, too.

Eric put his hands in his pockets, lifted one foot, and hopped. The monkey didn't have pockets. But he put his hands at his sides, lifted a foot, and hopped many times in a big circle around the cage. Then the monkey sat on the floor of the cage, on top of a banana peel. The monkey rubbed his stomach and made a funny, laughing sound.

"Your monkey hops better than you do," Billy said.

"Do something else," Cam told Eric.

Eric scratched his nose. The monkey scratched his nose. Eric clapped his hands and jumped. The monkey did that, too.

"Now, I'll do something the monkey can't do," Eric said.

Eric held his hands over his head. He leaned forward, took a little jump, and stood on his hands. Eric walked like that, upside down. Then he fell to the floor.

Eric looked up at the monkey cage. The very small monkey looked at Eric and smiled. Then the monkey stood on his hands and ran around the cage. Using his tail, he pulled himself onto a swing and made that funny, laughing sound again.

Eric began to laugh. Cam and Billy laughed, too.

"That monkey walks on his hands better than you do," Cam said. "He hops and scratches his nose better, too. But I'll bet you're better at spelling and long division."

"I'm not so sure," Billy said. "Some monkeys are very smart."

Cam put her arm around Eric's shoulder. As they walked out of the monkey

12

house, Cam said, "Well, no monkey is as smart as my friend Eric."

Billy followed Cam and Eric out of the monkey house. There was a small crowd near the seal pool. Cam, Eric, and Billy went there to see what was happening.

It was feeding time for the seals. A woman was standing at the edge of the pool holding a bucket filled with small fish. The woman threw the fish to the seals. The seals caught some of the fish with their mouths. The other fish landed in the pool, and the seals swam to get them.

A baby seal was sitting on a large rock. It tried to reach the fish that landed nearby. But one of the bigger seals always got there first.

"Oh, give the baby something to eat," a man in the crowd called out.

The woman threw some fish to the other side of the pool. The big seals all swam after them. Then the woman threw a few

14

fish to the rock for the baby seal.

When her bucket was empty, the woman left the seal pool. Many of the people who had come to watch walked away.

"Let's go to the reptile house. I want to see the alligators," Billy said. "My father is a dentist, and whenever he sees an alligator he says, 'Just look at those teeth.'"

As Cam, Eric, and Billy walked toward the reptile house, they passed a gift shop. They went inside. Billy bought a poster of a smiling alligator. Cam bought a banner. Eric found a book about monkeys.

Eric gave the book to the man behind the counter. The man put the book into a bag. Eric reached into his pocket for his wallet. Then he reached into his other pants pocket.

"Come on, pay the man," Billy said.

"I can't! My wallet is gone!"

Chapter Three

"Are you sure you had your wallet with you?" Billy asked.

"I had it when I paid for the bus ride. And I had it when I paid the entrance fee to the zoo," Eric said.

Cam closed her eyes and said, "*Click.*"

"At the zoo entrance you put the wallet in your left pants pocket," Cam said. Then she opened her eyes.

Eric reached into his pockets again. Both pockets were empty.

Cam closed her eyes. She said, "*Click*" a

few times. Then she opened her eyes and said to Eric, "Come with me. I think I know where to find your wallet."

Eric and Billy followed Cam out of the gift shop. They had to run to keep up with her.

"Where are we going?" Billy asked.

"To the monkey house," Eric said, and pointed to the large brick building ahead. "I'll bet Cam thinks my wallet fell out when I was walking on my hands."

Honk! Honk!

18

Cam, Eric, and Billy stopped to let a gardener's truck filled with dirt pass. Then they went into the monkey house.

Cam, Eric, and Billy looked on the floor of the monkey house. Cam looked up. She looked into one of the monkey cages. Then she ran outside.

"I found it. I found my wallet," Eric said. He opened it. "And the money is still here."

Billy walked over to Eric. He looked at the wallet. Then Billy and Eric looked at each other, and they both said, "Where's Cam?"

Eric and Billy ran toward the monkey house door just as Cam was coming in.

"I found my wallet," Eric told Cam.

"They're gone," Cam said.

"Who's gone?" Eric asked.

"The monkeys! The cage was full of monkeys, and now it's almost empty!"

Cam led Eric and Billy to the first monkey cage. Eric's monkey and a few of the other monkeys were missing.

"I think someone stole them," Cam said.

Billy shook his head and told Cam, "No one would steal monkeys. The zoo keeper is probably feeding them somewhere. Or maybe the monkeys are being moved to another cage."

"No," Cam said and shook her head. "The monkeys are fed in their cage. Look. There are even some banana peels in there from the last feeding. And if they were moving the monkeys, they would have taken them all."

Then Eric asked, "Where would they move monkeys? *This* is the monkey house."

"Let's tell one of the guards," Cam said.

Cam and Eric ran out of the monkey house. Billy walked slowly after them. Cam stood on a bench and looked around. Then she jumped down and ran toward the lion cage. Eric and Billy followed her.

A tall, fat guard with a big moustache was standing there. His arms were folded.

"He looks like a walrus," Billy whispered
to Eric.

"Someone stole a bunch of monkeys,"
Cam told the guard.

The guard looked down at Cam and
smiled. "No one stole any monkeys," he said.

He turned and pointed to a padlock on the door of the lion's cage and said, "No one can open a cage without a key."

The guard folded his arms again. Cam, Eric, and Billy walked away.

Cam and Eric were quiet as they walked back to the monkey house. But Billy wasn't. "I knew the monkeys weren't stolen," he said. "How could anyone steal a bunch of monkeys? I knew they weren't stolen."

While Cam and Eric looked inside the monkey house, Billy sat on the bench. He kept saying, "I knew they weren't stolen."

Cam and Eric looked on the floor near the first cage.

Cam whispered to Eric, "That guard would have told us if the zoo moved the monkeys. I still think they were stolen."

Billy looked at the monkeys in the other cages. And he read the signs describing the monkeys.

Cam and Eric walked outside. They

looked into the first cage. Then Cam saw something on the ground nearby. She picked it up and said, "Look at this. Now I *know* those monkeys were stolen."

Chapter Four

Cam was holding a padlock. The top of it had been cut. Cam ran toward the lion's cage.

"Wait," Eric called as he ran after Cam. "The monkey cage *has* a lock."

But Cam didn't wait. She ran right up to the guard, held out the lock, and said, "Look at this!"

The guard looked down at Cam and the lock. Then he looked up again.

"This is the monkey cage lock. Someone cut it and stole the monkeys," Cam said.

Eric pulled on Cam's sleeve and whispered to her, "That's not it."

"Try your key in this," Cam told the guard.

The guard looked down at Cam again. Then he pulled a large key ring from his pocket. He picked out one of the keys and said, "This key fits the locks on all the cages. But it won't fit that lock."

The guard took the lock from Cam. He put the key in. The key fit. The guard turned the key and the lock opened.

"Let's look at that cage," the guard said. He walked quickly to the monkey house. Cam and Eric had to run to keep up.

"Whoever stole those monkeys put another lock on the cage door," Cam said, as she ran alongside the guard.

The guard looked at the lock on the outside door of the first monkey cage. He tried to put his key in. It didn't fit. He went inside the monkey house and picked up the telephone.

Billy rushed over to Cam and Eric. "What's he doing here?" he asked Cam.

"Shh," Eric said.

"This is Senior Guard Wally Russell," he said into the telephone. "Someone switched the locks on one of the monkey cages. And some monkeys are missing."

The guard listened for a short while.

Then he said, "Yes, I'll wait here."

The guard looked into the first cage. Billy was right behind him. "I knew those monkeys were stolen," Billy told the guard. "I just knew it."

Cam and Eric were standing by the door to the monkey house. "How could someone sneak a bunch of monkeys out of a zoo?" Cam asked.

Cam stood there looking out. At the far end of the path, she saw two guards running toward the monkey house. Behind them was another guard riding a small cart.

"That's it!" Cam said. "Come with me."

Cam and Eric ran out of the monkey house. They ran past the guards to the wide paved road near the zoo entrance. Cam stopped near a small boy and a man who were looking at a map.

"Did you see an ice-cream cart go past here?" Cam asked.

"No," the boy said. "But we did see one

when we were looking at the animals with
four legs and the real long necks."

Cam closed her eyes and said, *"Click."*
Then she said, "Come on, Eric. The giraffes are right down this road."

Cam started to run off again.

"Stop! Just stop," Eric called out. "I ran with you to get the guard and I ran back to the monkey house. I did that twice. Then I ran here. I'm not running anyplace else unless you tell me what's going on."

Cam stopped. She turned and told Eric,

"When I saw the guard riding a cart, I knew where the monkeys were. They're in an ice-cream cart. Those ice-cream men ride all over the zoo. And if you take the ice cream out, there's room in one of those carts for two or three monkeys."

"Maybe one of the guards with carts stole the monkeys," Eric said.

Cam shook her head. "The guards have keys. A guard wouldn't have to cut the lock."

"But how will we get to see if the ice-cream man has any monkeys in his cart?" Eric asked.

"We can listen for strange noises coming out of the cart. Or we can tell the man we want to buy some ice cream. I'll bet he says, 'Sorry, I'm all out.' "

Cam smiled and asked Eric, "Will you come with me now?"

Eric nodded and they ran together toward the giraffes.

Chapter Five

Cam and Eric ran down the main road. They ran past the camel rides and the elephants to the giraffes' cage. They found the ice-cream cart still there. The man was sitting on a bench and reading.

"We'd like to buy some ice cream," Cam said.

The man closed his book. "I have 'Piggy Back' cones. That's a cone with two scoops of ice cream. You can get rum raisin and strawberry or chocolate and lemon."

"Yuck," Eric said. "What horrible flavors."

Cam leaned close to Eric and whispered, "He doesn't really have any ice cream in there. He thinks by telling us those horrible flavors we'll say, 'No thanks.'"

"I'll take a chocolate and lemon cone," Cam told the man.

"And I'll take rum raisin and strawberry," Eric said.

The man opened the small door to his cart. He reached in and took out two cones.

"That's seventy-five cents each," he said, as he gave Cam and Eric the cones and two napkins.

Cam and Eric paid the man. Then Eric tasted the ice cream.

"Yuck," Eric said again. "This stuff is terrible!"

"That must be the rum raisin," the man said. "Everyone hates that flavor."

Cam asked, "Are there any other ice-cream carts in the zoo?"

"Well, yes. There's one near the zebras and another near the reptiles. But we all have the same flavors."

Cam said, "*Click*," and closed her eyes. Then she said, "The zebras are all the way at the end of this road, right past the camels and the bison."

Cam and Eric walked quickly down the road. When they came to a trash can Eric stopped. He held his ice-cream cone over the can and shook it gently.

"What are you doing?" Cam asked.

"I'm trying to shake off the rum raisin scoop without losing the strawberry."

Cam took the top scoop off of Eric's cone and dropped it into the trash. Cam wiped her fingers on her napkin and said, "Let's go."

The ice-cream vendor was sitting on a bench near the zebras. She was sleeping with her feet resting on the ice-cream cart.

"She doesn't look like someone who has just stolen some monkeys," Eric told Cam.

"Shh," Cam whispered. She crawled to the ice-cream cart. She put her ear next to it and listened. Eric put his ear against the side of the cart and listened, too.

"I don't hear any monkeys in there," Eric whispered.

"Neither do I," Cam whispered.

"All you'll hear in there is ice cream," someone said in a loud voice. "And ice cream doesn't talk."

Cam and Eric looked up and saw the ice-
cream woman standing there.

Eric stood and told the woman, "Some
monkeys are missing. We thought they
might be inside your ice-cream cart."

"Monkeys! What I have in here is worse

than monkeys," the woman said as she opened the small door. "I have chocolate and lemon, and rum raisin and strawberry ice cream. I haven't sold a cone all day."

Cam licked her ice-cream cone and said, "It does taste pretty bad."

The woman closed the small door and sat on the bench again. She put her feet on the cart. "Monkeys!" she said, and laughed as she closed her eyes.

There was a trash can nearby. Cam dropped the lemon ice cream into the trash. She took a few quick bites and finished the chocolate and the cone.

Cam and Eric walked toward the reptile house to find the third ice-cream cart. They walked past a pond. A man was standing there and throwing bread crumbs to the ducks and geese.

Quack, quack, honk, honk, the ducks and geese called as they chased after the bread crumbs.

Cam watched the ducks and geese eat the crumbs. She listened to the sounds they made. Then she closed her eyes and said, "*Click.*" She said "*click*" again.

Cam opened her eyes and told Eric, "I know just where those monkeys are. And they're not inside an ice-cream cart."

Chapter Six

"The honking sounds those geese made helped me solve the mystery," Cam told Eric, as they quickly walked along the main road. Then Cam saw that a crowd had gathered at the main entrance to the zoo. She ran ahead.

Eric took one last big bite and finished his ice-cream cone. Then he ran to catch up with Cam.

"Where have you been?" Billy asked, as he came out to meet Cam and Eric. "You missed everything. The zoo director and lots more guards came. Five monkeys were stolen."

"I know where they are. I know who took them," Cam said.

Cam found Senior Guard Wally Russell and told him, "I know who stole the monkeys."

A short, fat man with a beard and thick eyeglasses was talking to a few of the guards. He turned and asked Cam, "How do you know who took them?"

"This is the girl I told you about," Wally Russell told the man. "She's the one who found the lock."

"I'm Don Cooper. I'm the director of the zoo," the man said, as he shook hands with Cam and Eric. "Now what can you tell me about the monkeys?"

"Some people drove in here with a truck. The back of the truck was filled with dirt. I thought they were doing some planting. But the truck passed us later. It was leaving the zoo and the back was still filled with dirt."

"We're not doing any planting. That truck didn't belong here," Mr. Cooper said. He walked quickly to the entrance and asked the guard if the truck rode past.

"About fifteen minutes ago," the guard said.

Cam described the truck. Mr. Cooper called the police. He told them about the monkeys and the truck.

Mr. Cooper stood by the telephone. He

folded and unfolded his arms. He put his hands into his jacket pockets and took them out. Then he clapped his hands and said, "Come on. I can't just wait here. Maybe we can find that truck."

Cam, Eric, Billy, and Wally Russell followed Mr. Cooper to the parking lot. Mr. Cooper opened the doors to an old green car. The backseat was filled with baby toys, balls, and dolls.

"Just push those aside," Mr. Cooper said. "I use them when I play with the baby animals."

Cam and Wally Russell sat on the front seat next to Mr. Cooper. Eric and Billy sat in the back.

As the car went through the gate, Cam said, "When the geese honked they reminded me of the truck. It honked at us twice."

Billy said, "Did you know that some people keep geese as pets?"

"And I thought it was strange," Cam went on, "for that truck to bring dirt into the zoo and take it out again."

Mr. Cooper stopped just outside the zoo. There was a long line of cars ahead of him. Mr. Cooper waited. The traffic light at the end of the road was red. But when the light turned to green, the cars still didn't move. Mr. Cooper honked his car horn.

"It happens every time," Mr. Cooper said. "When I'm in a rush, there's a traffic jam."

The light turned red. Then it turned green again, but no cars moved.

"What's going on up there?" Mr. Cooper asked, as he got out of his car and walked down the road. Cam and Eric followed him. And right behind them were Billy and Wally Russell.

There had been an accident. A small blue car had crashed into a large truck. The drivers were standing in the middle of the road and arguing.

"That's it," Cam said. "That's the truck I saw in the zoo!"

Chapter Seven

A police siren sounded. The siren got louder and louder. Then two police cars turned the corner. Mr. Cooper waved his arms and the second car stopped.

"We can't help you," the officer said as he rolled down his window. "Some zoo animals have been stolen."

"I know. I called you. I'm Don Cooper, the director of the zoo. And I think we've found the thieves."

The police officer opened his car door and got out. Mr. Cooper told him the truck had been in the zoo at the time the monkeys were stolen.

The police officer walked over to the truck. Mr. Cooper, Cam, Eric, Billy, and Wally Russell were right behind the officer.

"Whose truck is this?" the officer asked.

"It's mine," a young man said. He was wearing a green baseball hat and a sweat shirt. "And she crashed into me." The young man pointed to a woman standing next to the small blue car. "My neck hurts. And my back hurts. And my truck is dented."

"You were turning?" the officer asked.

"Yes, and that woman crashed right into me. She shouldn't be allowed to drive a car."

"If you were turning and she was going straight," the officer said, "she had the right of way."

The woman said, "He wants me to fix his truck and pay for his bad back. But if I had the right of way, the accident wasn't my fault."

The woman looked at her car for dents or scratches. She didn't find any so she got into her car and drove away.

The young man walked toward his truck. "Wait just a minute," the officer told him. "I want to talk to you about some monkeys."

The man turned. "I don't know anything about monkeys," he said.

"Then you won't mind if I look around," the police officer said.

He opened the truck door and looked

inside. Mr. Cooper looked, too. They walked around the truck. Cam, Eric, Billy, and Wally Russell followed them. They all bent down and looked under the truck. They looked in the back of the truck, but they didn't find any monkeys.

"Can I go now?" the young man asked.

The officer nodded. The young man climbed into the truck.

"Hurry," Eric whispered to Cam. "Say '*Click.*' Do something!"

Cam closed her eyes and said "*Click*" just as the truck started to move. The traffic light was red. The truck waited. Cam said "*Click*" again. Then the light turned green.

"Wait!" Cam called out as she opened her eyes. "I know where he has those monkeys hidden."

The police officer blew his whistle and ran to the truck. "Pull over to the side of the road," he said.

"Look at the sticks in the back of the

truck," Cam told the police officer. "I'll bet they're hollow. That's so the monkeys can breathe. They're in a cage under the dirt."

The police officer and Wally Russell dug their hands into the dirt. "Hey, there's a cloth here. And there's something under the cloth. It feels like a cage."

Mr. Cooper opened two latches at the back of the truck. The gate dropped down and he found his monkeys.

Mr. Cooper and Wally Russell pulled the cage out and put it on top of the dirt. There were holes in the top of the cage. Attached to each hole was a wooden tube.

Mr. Cooper looked closely at each of the monkeys. Cam, Eric, and Billy looked at them, too. Eric scratched his nose and put his hands behind his back as he looked. One of the monkeys scratched his nose. Then he put his hands behind his back. It was the very small monkey, the one that had copied Eric.

Chapter Eight

The young man with the green baseball hat drove his truck back to the zoo. Wally Russell rode with him. The police officer and Mr. Cooper followed in their cars. Cam, Eric, and Billy rode with Mr. Cooper.

"How did you know where to find the monkeys?" Mr. Cooper asked Cam.

"I had lots of pictures of that truck stored in my head. I looked at them and saw that the rakes and the shovels in the back had been moved around. But the sticks hadn't. They were in the exact same places each time."

50

"That wouldn't happen if the sticks were not attached to the cage," Eric said. "If the sticks were in a pile of dirt they would move around when the truck moved."

"If you have pictures stored in your head," Mr. Cooper said, "you must have a photographic memory."

"She does," Eric said.

"Well, your memory saved the zoo some valuable monkeys."

"I have a good memory, too," Billy said.

Mr. Cooper drove his car through the main entrance. He parked right outside the monkey house. The truck, two police cars, and three police officers were already there.

Mr. Cooper and Wally Russell carried the box from the truck to the first cage. The young man with the green hat had the key to the lock on the first cage. He opened it. Mr. Cooper opened the box. "Go on," he told the monkeys. "Get into your cage." But the monkeys didn't move.

Mr. Cooper took a few bananas from the trunk of his car. He threw them into the cage and the monkeys went in after them. Mr. Cooper put one of the zoo's locks on the cage door. Then he turned to the young man and asked, "Tell me, what did you plan to do with those monkeys?"

"I was going to sell them," he answered, keeping his head down. "I know some people who would pay a lot of money to buy a pet monkey."

The young man got back into his truck. A police officer got in with him. Then he drove off with one police car riding ahead of him and the other following him.

"You children deserve some reward for saving our monkeys," Mr. Cooper said. "I'll give each of you free passes to the zoo. I'm going to take you someplace that isn't open to most people. And I have something really special to give you."

Mr. Cooper gave Cam, Eric, and Billy free passes to the zoo. Then the children followed Mr. Cooper to a building near the zoo entrance.

"This is the zoo kitchen," Mr. Cooper said. He led them into a large room. "This is where we prepare the food for all the animals."

The children watched as large "hamburgers" were being made for the lions.

"We mix vitamins and minerals in with different kinds of meat," Mr. Cooper said.

Cam, Eric, and Billy watched as salads were made for the apes and monkeys. They saw live insects, mice, and chickens that were kept in the kitchen to feed the snakes, lizards, and alligators.

"Now," Mr. Cooper said, "it's time for your special treat."

Cam, Eric, and Billy followed him to a bench outside the reptile house. A woman was sitting there reading. And she was holding onto the handle of an ice-cream cart.

"We have a great flavor of ice cream here," Mr. Cooper said. "It's one of my favorites. Lemon."

"Give each of these children a lemon and chocolate cone," Mr. Cooper told the woman.

"No, thank you," Cam and Eric said.

"Well," Mr. Cooper said, "I'm sure you'll want to taste my other favorite flavor of ice cream."

"No, thank you," Cam and Eric said again.

"But you don't even know what flavor it is."

"Oh, yes, we do," Cam and Eric said, and laughed. "Rum raisin."

Cam, Eric, Billy, and Mr. Cooper walked back to the monkey house. As they walked, Cam and Eric watched Billy and Mr. Cooper eat their lemon and chocolate ice-cream cones.

Billy smiled whenever Mr. Cooper looked at him. But when Mr. Cooper wasn't looking, Billy made a funny face, like he was eating poison.

When they came to the monkey house, Mr. Cooper looked into the first cage. "They look happy to be back home," he said.

Eric and Billy also looked into the monkey cage.

"Let me take a picture of you," Cam said.

Eric, Billy, and Mr. Cooper turned to face Cam. They smiled. Cam closed her eyes and said, "*Click.*"

Eric turned and saw the smallest monkey look straight at Cam. The monkey blinked his eyes, and Eric said "*Click.*" Cam opened her eyes.

"Hey," Billy said. "That monkey said, '*Click.*' I'll bet he has a great memory, too."

Eric laughed. He put his arm around Cam's shoulder and said, "Well, no monkey has as good a memory as my friend Cam!"